Dear Parents and Educators,

Welcome to Penguin Young Readers! As parents and educators, you know that each child develops at his or her own pace—in terms of speech, critical thinking, and, of course, reading. Penguin Young Readers recognizes this fact. As a result, each Penguin Young Readers book is assigned a traditional easy-to-read level (1–4) as well as a Guided Reading Level (A–P). Both of these systems will help you choose the right book for your child. Please refer to the back of each book for specific leveling information. Penguin Young Readers features esteemed authors and illustrators, stories about favorite characters, fascinating nonfiction, and more!

Cat Show

LEVEL **2**

GUIDED READING LEVEL **F**

This book is perfect for a **Progressing Reader** who:
- can figure out unknown words by using picture and context clues;
- can recognize beginning, middle, and ending sounds;
- can make and confirm predictions about what will happen in the text; and
- can distinguish between fiction and nonfiction.

Here are some **activities** you can do during and after reading this book:
- Sight Words: Sight words are frequently used words that readers must know just by looking at them. These words are known instantly, on sight. Knowing these words helps children develop into efficient readers. As you read the story, point out the sight words below.

are	four	here	play	three
big	get	must	some	want
blue	have	now	there	will

- Discuss the different ways the kids in this story sort the cats. On a separate sheet of paper, make a list of the categories they used (for example, size). Can you think of other ways to sort the cats?

Remember, sharing the love of reading with a child is the best gift you can give!

—Bonnie Bader, EdM
  Penguin Young Readers program

*Penguin Young Readers are leveled by independent reviewers applying the standards developed by Irene Fountas and Gay Su Pinnell in *Matching Books to Readers: Using Leveled Books in Guided Reading*, Heinemann, 1999.

To all of my family and friends, with love—TP

Penguin Young Readers
Published by the Penguin Group
Penguin Group (USA) Inc., 375 Hudson Street, New York, New York 10014, USA
Penguin Group (Canada), 90 Eglinton Avenue East, Suite 700, Toronto, Ontario M4P 2Y3, Canada
(a division of Pearson Penguin Canada Inc.)
Penguin Books Ltd., 80 Strand, London WC2R 0RL, England
Penguin Group Ireland, 25 St. Stephen's Green, Dublin 2, Ireland (a division of Penguin Books Ltd.)
Penguin Group (Australia), 250 Camberwell Road, Camberwell, Victoria 3124, Australia
(a division of Pearson Australia Group Pty. Ltd.)
Penguin Books India Pvt. Ltd., 11 Community Centre, Panchsheel Park, New Delhi—110 017, India
Penguin Group (NZ), 67 Apollo Drive, Rosedale, Auckland 0632, New Zealand
(a division of Pearson New Zealand Ltd.)
Penguin Books (South Africa) (Pty.) Ltd., 24 Sturdee Avenue,
Rosebank, Johannesburg 2196, South Africa

Penguin Books Ltd., Registered Offices: 80 Strand, London WC2R 0RL, England

Text copyright © 2003 by Tracey West. Illustrations copyright © 2003 by Tamara Petrosino. All rights reserved. First published in 2003 by Grosset & Dunlap, an imprint of Penguin Group (USA) Inc. Published in 2012 by Penguin Young Readers, an imprint of Penguin Group (USA) Inc., 345 Hudson Street, New York, New York 10014. Manufactured in China.

Library of Congress Control Number: 2002015626

ISBN 978-0-448-43112-3   10 9 8 7 6 5 4 3 2

by Jayne Harvey
illustrated by Tamara Petrosino

Penguin Young Readers
An Imprint of Penguin Group (USA) Inc.

It is time for the cat show.

The kids must get the cats
ready for the show.

Their parents will be here soon.

How will the kids group the cats?

Pam thinks of a way

to sort the cats.

Some cats are big.

Some cats are small.

The cats are in groups.

There are seven big cats.

There are three small cats.

Oh no!

Some of the small cats

want to play.

Matt thinks of another way

to sort the cats.

Some cats

have stripes.

Some cats

have no stripes.

The cats are in groups.

There are four cats

with stripes.

There are six cats

without stripes.

15

Oh no!

Some of the striped cats

want to fight!

Jake thinks of another way
to sort the cats.

Some cats have

blue eyes.

Some cats have

green eyes.

The cats are in groups.

There are five cats

with green eyes.

There are five cats

with blue eyes.

Oh no!

Some of the cats

with green eyes

want to run around.

Will thinks of another way

to sort the cats.

Some cats have gray fur.

Some cats have orange fur.

Some cats have black fur.

Some cats have white fur.

The cats are in groups.

There are four cats

with gray fur.

There are three cats

with orange fur.

There are two cats

with black fur.

There is one cat

with white fur.

Oh no!

Some of the gray cats

want to make noise.

Kim thinks of another way

to sort the cats.

One cat has a hat.

Some cats have no hats.

The cats are in groups.

There is one cat with a hat.

There are nine cats with no hats.

There is one mouse.

One mouse?

The cats chase the mouse.

The kids chase the cats.

The cats are tired.

Now the cats are

in one big group.

All 10 cats are asleep.

The sleeping cats are so cute.

The parents are very proud.

The cat show is a hit!